PUFFIN BOOKS

The Roman
Giant

D0800106

The Romantic Giant

Kaye Umansky

Illustrated by
Doffy Weir

PUFFIN BOOKS

PUFFIN BOOKS

Published by the Penguin Group
Penguin Books Ltd, 27 Wrights Lane, London W8 5TZ, England
Penguin Books USA Inc., 375 Hudson Street, New York, New York 10014, USA
Penguin Books Australia Ltd, Ringwood, Victoria, Australia
Penguin Books Canada Ltd, 10 Alcorn Avenue, Toronto, Ontario, Canada M4V 3B2
Penguin Books (NZ) Ltd, 182–190 Wairau Road, Auckland 10, New Zealand

Penguin Books Ltd, Registered Offices: Harmondsworth, Middlesex, England

First published by Hamish Hamilton Ltd 1994
Published in Puffin Books 1997
1 3 5 7 9 10 8 6 4 2

Text copyright © Kaye Umansky, 1994
Illustrations copyright © Doffy Weir, 1994
All rights reserved

The moral right of the author and illustrator has been asserted

Filmset in Plantin

Made and printed in Hong Kong by Imago Publishing Limited

Waldo the giant was in love. His dream girl
was the beautiful Princess Clarissa, who
lived in the palace down in the valley and
whose picture he had seen in a magazine.
She had golden curls, periwinkle blue eyes
and a cute little upturned nose which made
Waldo go weak at the knees.

He showed the picture to Heavy Hetty,
his next-door neighbour.

Heavy Hetty was a wrestler. She didn't
say much, but her biceps were amazing.

"Look!" he said. "Look at the hair!
Look at the eyes! Look at that nose! Isn't
she beautiful?"

Hetty put down the rock she was
squeezing and looked.

"Too small," she grunted. "Couldn't wrestle for toffee. Probably only comes up to your knee."

"So?" said Waldo. "Love conquers all. I'm going to marry her and bring her to live up here."

"She's used to a palace. She won't like your cave."

"I'll decorate it," promised Waldo. "I'll put in a proper kitchen."

"Suit yourself," shrugged Hetty, picking up her rock. "But personally, I reckon you're not her type. Too big. Too hairy. Not romantic enough."

"I don't care," said Waldo stubbornly. "Opposites attract. I love her. And I *am* romantic. You'll see."

And he went back to his cave to write a poem.

The next morning he showed it to Hetty.
He waited impatiently while she finished
her push-ups, then thrust it under her nose.

Hetty read it as she towelled down. It
was decorated with little hearts, and read:

Roses are red, daisies are white,
Princess Clarissa's a bit of all right.

"Well! What d'you think?" asked Waldo anxiously. "Is it meaningful? Does it get over what I'm trying to say? I've been working on it all night."

"It's OK," growled Hetty, thumping her   punchbag.

"Really? Then I'll post it off straight away. I'm sure to get a reply soon."

But he didn't. A whole week went by, and there was no reply from the palace.

"It must have got lost in the post," Waldo told Hetty, who was out breaking rocks. "So I've sent her a box of chocolates instead," he added. "I put a message inside. I put *From Your Biggest Admirer*. She's sure to get those, because they went

by recorded delivery. I expect she'll send me a perfumed thank-you note and invite me to tea by candlelight. I say, mind out, Het! That club came a bit too close to my foot for comfort."

He was wrong. Although the chocolates went by recorded delivery, there was still no word from Clarissa.

When another whole week had gone by, Waldo was desperate. He had run out of trees to carve *W luvs PC* on. Clarissa's picture had fallen to pieces as a result of so much anxious folding and unfolding.

He went to find Hetty, who was out jogging up the mountain.

"I can't understand it," he panted mournfully, struggling to keep up. "She must know how much I feel about her. Why doesn't she reply? I'm running out of romantic ideas."

"Flowers?" suggested Hetty, leaping a small precipice. "I've heard even stunted girls like flowers."

"Good idea!" cried Waldo joyfully. "I'll pick her a bunch right now. And then I shall go down to the palace and deliver it myself. That way I'll know she gets it. And – oh! Maybe I'll get to see her! Speak to her, even!"

Hetty watched him go crashing off down the slope. She gave a little sigh, then began to work on her pectorals.

Much, much later that day, aching
slightly from an hour of sheep juggling, she
was drinking cocoa in her cave when there
came a knocking at the front boulder.
Hetty rolled it aside, and there stood
Waldo.

"Oh, it's you," said Hetty. "Well? Did
she like the flowers?"

"I don't know," confessed Waldo, shaking his head sadly. "I didn't get beyond the front gate. The place was awash with soldiers for some reason. I asked the Captain of the Guard to give them to her, but I don't know if he did. He was

very curt. I waited around for ages, but
she didn't come out and say thank you."

"I'd give up," advised Hetty.

"Give up? Never! Why, that girl gives me
a spring in my step and a song in my
heart!"

"Sing to her, then," snapped Hetty. "Go
down there now and sing in the moonlight.
Serenade her under her balcony. But don't
expect me to wait up."

"Het," said Waldo. "Het, you're a
genius."

And for the second time that day, he
went crashing off down the mountain,
pausing only to call into his cave to collect
his guitar.

An hour or so later, he was back again.

"What happened?" asked Hetty, who
had waited up. "Did you sing?"

"Yes," said Waldo. "I sang. I sang 'Ten Green Bottles'. It's the only one I know from start to finish."

"Well? Did she come out? Not that I'm interested."

"Yes," sighed Waldo. "She came out. And so did her mum and dad and the Captain Of The Guard."

"And what did they say?"

"They told me to clear off," admitted Waldo.

"They said I was a thundering great pest. But, you know what, Het? I didn't care. That Clarissa's nothing like her picture. Up close, her nose is horrible. And she's got this squeaky little voice. And you were right.

She only comes up to my knee. Much, much
too small."

"I told you that to begin with," said
Hetty.

"I know," said Waldo sheepishly. Then:

"Doing anything tomorrow night, Het?" he asked.

"Working out," said Hetty.

"Mind if I join you?" asked Waldo. "I'll bring my own weights. We could do a bit of arm-wrestling, maybe. By candlelight."

"Oh, Waldo," said Hetty, with a little blush. "You're so romantic."

Also available in First Young Puffin

BLESSU
Dick King-Smith

The tall, flowering elephant-grasses give Blessu
hay-fever. 'BLESS YOU!' all the elephants cry
whenever little Blessu sneezes, which is very often.
Blessu grows slowly except for one part of
him – his trunk – and his sneeze becomes the
biggest, loudest sneeze in the world!

WHAT STELLA SAW
Wendy Smith

Stella's mum is a fortune-teller who always gets things
wrong. But when football-mad Stella starts reading
tea-leaves, she seems to be right every time!
Or is she . . .

THE DAY THE SMELLS WENT WRONG
Catherine Sefton

It is just an ordinary day, but Jackie and Phil can't
understand why nothing smells as it should. Toast
smells like tar, fruit smells like fish, and their school
dinners smell of perfume! Together, Jackie and Phil
discover the cause of the problem . . .